STICK DOG

Praise for the STICK DOG series

"Full of silly, slapstick doggy humor.
An enticing package."
—*Kirkus Reviews*

"Readers are sure to enjoy this adorable story
about working together toward a goal."
—ALA *Booklist*

"Will be a sure hit with children."
— *School Library Journal*

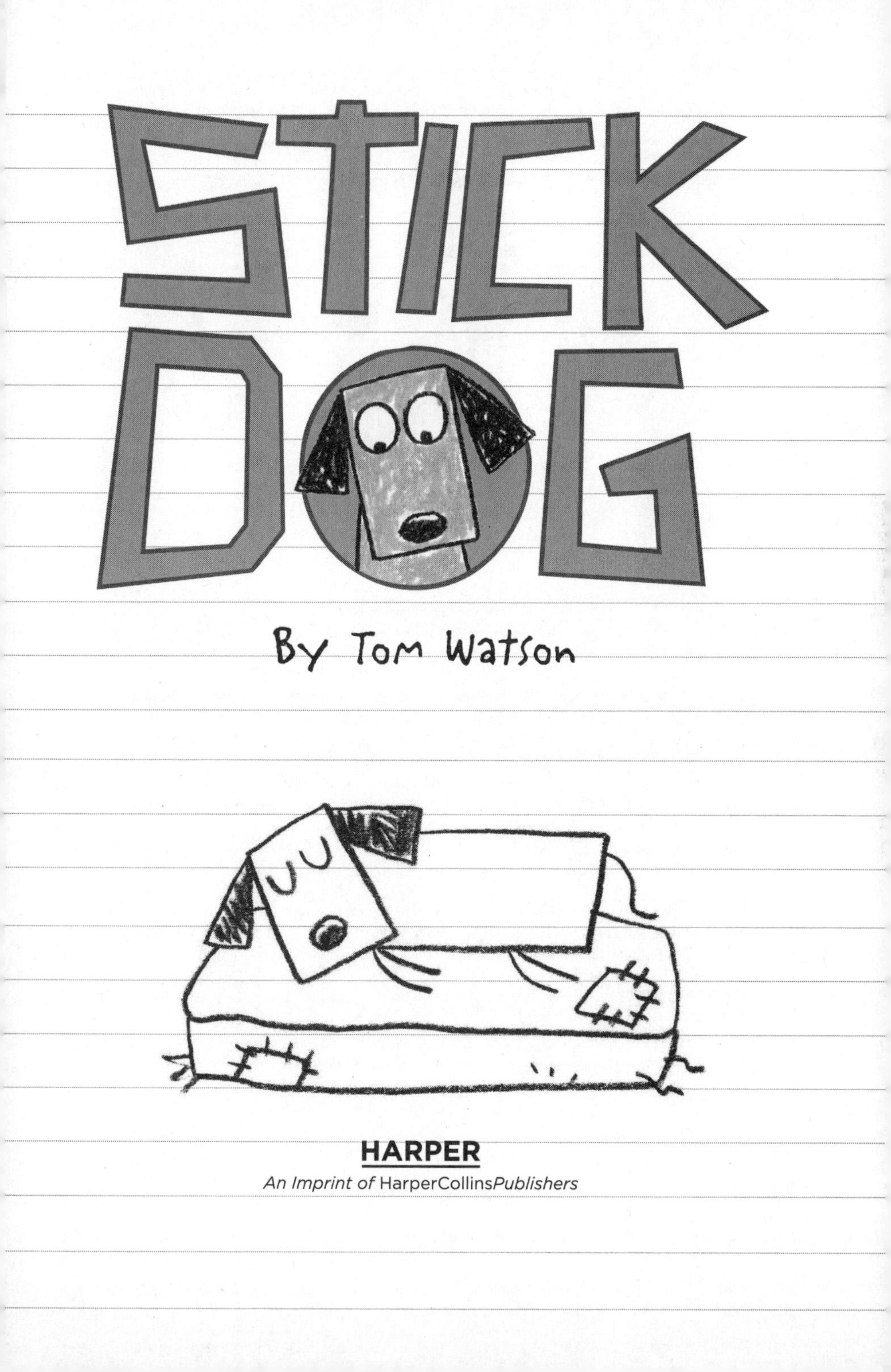

By Tom Watson

HARPER
An Imprint of HarperCollins*Publishers*

Dedicated to Mary

(SDLMM)

Stick Dog

Illustrations by Ethan Long based on original sketches by Tom Watson

www.harpercollinschildrens.com

Library of Congress Cataloging-in-Publication Data

Watson, Tom.
Stick dog / by Tom Watson. — 1st ed.
p. cm.
Summary: "Stick Dog and his four friends—Stripes, Mutt, Poo-Poo, and Karen—will do anything to steal some sweet-smelling hamburgers from a family at Picasso Park!"— Provided by publisher.
ISBN 978-0-06-226435-0 (pbk.)
[1. Dogs—Fiction. 2. Humorous stories.] I. Title.
PZ7.W3298Sti 2013 2012019093
[Fic]—dc23 CIP
AC

Typography by Tom Starace

20 21 22 23 24 PC/LSCH 10 9 8 7 6 5 4 3

❖

First paperback edition, 2020

TABLE OF CONTENTS

Chapter 1
I CAN'T DRAW, OKAY?

This is Stick Dog.

He is not called Stick Dog because he likes sticks. Although, now that I think about it, he does like sticks. All dogs like sticks, don't they? I mean, what kind of dog doesn't like sticks? If I came across an animal that looked like a dog and I offered it a stick and it refused to take it, then I might conclude that it's not a dog at all. Wouldn't you?

I would think it's a furry chair or something.

Anyway, Stick Dog is not called Stick Dog because he likes sticks. He's called Stick Dog because I don't know how to draw.

I mean, I do know how to draw—I just don't know how to draw very well. You know how to draw stick people, right? A circle for a head, add a couple of lines for arms and legs, and—SHAZAM!—you've

got a stick person. I do the same thing for dogs. And that's how our main character got his name.

So, this is Stick Dog.

When I showed this picture of a dog to my art teacher, she scrunched up her face. I don't know about your art teacher, but when my art teacher scrunches up her face, it's not a compliment.

Then she regained her composure, unscrunched her face, and said, "Dogs don't have right angles, Tom."

And I said, "Stick dogs do."

Then she said, "But if you draw stick dogs, all your dog drawings will look the same."

After she left my desk and walked over to congratulate Jack Krulewitch on drawing a far superior and lovely dog with lots of realistic curves, I decided to prove her wrong. I like proving people wrong. It comes naturally to me.

So these are some other drawings of dogs. As you can no doubt see, they do NOT

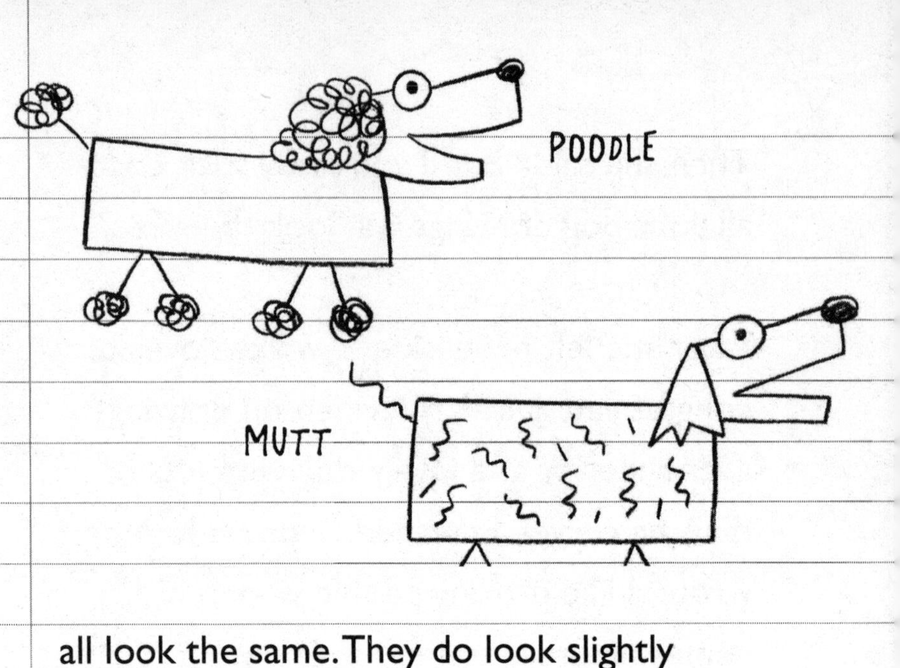

all look the same. They do look slightly similar, but with certain distinct features to tell them apart from Stick Dog himself. There's a Dalmatian, a poodle, and a dachshund.

There's also a mutt. Now, I couldn't figure out how to draw a mutt, which is a dog made up of many different breeds of dogs all mixed together. So he's that wavy dude up there. Because, really, a mutt can be just about anything, right? Big, small, long fur, short fur, curly—whatever. So wavy lines in the fur mean mutt. Got it?

I'm glad you get it. My art teacher didn't. When she came over to look at my drawings again, she scrunched up her face a second time.

She didn't unscrunch it. And that's just fine and dandy with me.

Okay, now before we start with the story, you and I need to agree on a few things.

First, you should know that it's not just dogs that I can't draw very well. I pretty much can't draw anything very well. I can't draw flowers, houses, candy bars,

asparagus, donkeys, caterpillars, airplanes, elbows, or French fries very well either. In fact, my asparagus stalks look a lot like my French fries. You should get the idea just from this example.

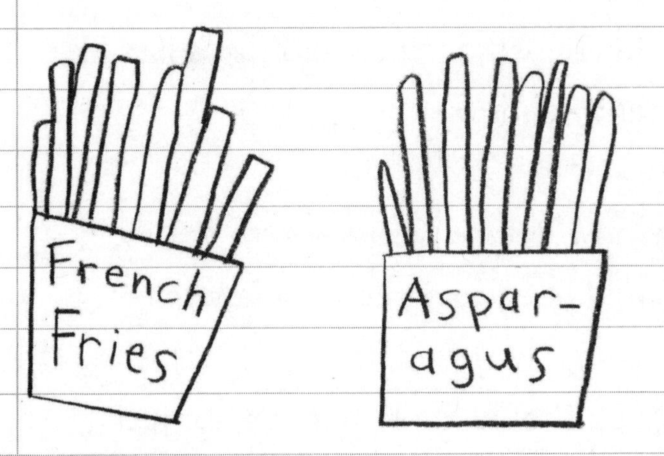

So, the first thing we have to agree on is this: I can't draw much of anything. Okay?

The second thing we have to agree on is: you're not going to give me any trouble about my drawing abilities. For instance, you're not allowed to say something like, "Dude, that drawing of a tree looks like a big thingy of broccoli."

Actually, trees and broccoli look a lot alike when you really think about it.

But, anyway, you get the point: I admit to you that I can't draw so well. And you promise that you won't hassle me about it.

Next, we need to talk about something my English teacher and I don't agree on. All of a sudden I'm realizing I often disagree with many of my teachers. I'm just like that, I guess.

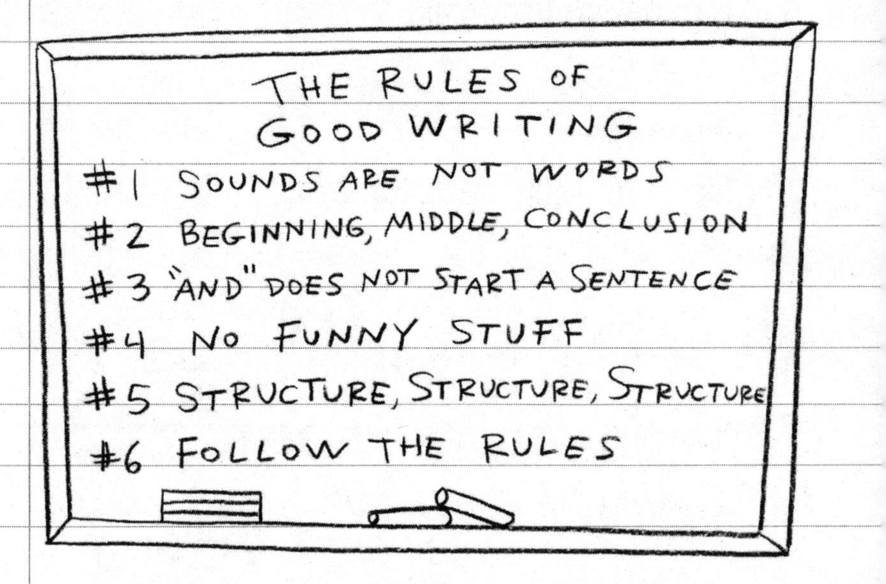

He likes to stand in front of class and say "Good writers follow good rules." He has lots of rules when it comes to writing. There have to be introductions and conclusions to everything, for instance. Sentences need to have proper structure. He says telling funny stories is for the campfire, not the classroom. He says starting sentences with the word "And" is unacceptable. He says never use sounds for words.

And, umm, yeah, he says a lot of other stuff.

When it comes to my English teacher's rules for writing, I'm reminded of a word my little sister made up when she found a worm in the yard: "barf-a-lucci."

While I have a feeling I'm not going to get very good grades for my Stick Dog stories, that doesn't matter when it comes to you and me and our agreement.

So the final thing we need to agree on is that this Stick Dog story (with the bad pictures that my art teacher doesn't like) will also be told in a way that I like (but my English teacher doesn't).

Good deal?

Excellent. Let's move on.

This is going to be fun.

Chapter 2

POO-POO, STRIPES, KAREN + MUTT

Stick Dog lives in the suburbs somewhere between Big City and the Forest. There are houses around, but there are also parks and playgrounds, swimming pools, streets, telephone poles, fire hydrants, and grassy lawns. He lives in a big, empty pipe that runs under Highway 16.

For as long as he can remember, this big pipe has been Stick Dog's home. And for as long as he can remember, he's always been alone. He's never lived with any other dogs. He's certainly never had a human family that he can remember.

This does not make Stick Dog sad at all. Maybe if he once had a human family or a brother or a sister and then suddenly found himself alone—well, then maybe he would feel sad living by himself in a big pipe out in the suburbs.

But he didn't—so he doesn't.

It is, after all, hard to miss something you've never had. For instance, I don't miss waking up on the moon and going for a gravity-defying morning stroll. Why?

Because I've never done it. But I bet astronauts who have actually walked on the moon probably miss bouncing around from crater to crater all the time.

See what I mean?

Besides, Stick Dog isn't really alone. He has some very good friends. We'll meet them in a couple of minutes.

There's no water in Stick Dog's pipe. It's nice and dry. And Stick Dog has decorated it with some of his favorite things. He sleeps on a comfy old couch cushion. He found it by a Dumpster behind a furniture store and dragged it home at night when nobody was watching. Stick Dog finds a lot of things this way.

Stick Dog also has a big assortment of things to chew on—mostly tennis balls and Frisbees that he's brought home from Picasso Park.

All in all, his pipe is a pretty good place to live.

He can hear crickets and toads at night.

And when the sky is clear, Stick Dog leans his head out of the end of his pipe and stares at the stars and the moon. On nights like that, lying there on his cushion with a Frisbee in his mouth, Stick Dog knows that he's got it pretty darn good.

So, Stick Dog has a nice place to live. And he's also got friends. Good friends. And what's better than a good friend? Well, maybe a good friend who happens to have some Doggie Snack-a-Roos in his pocket is a little better, but that's about it.

When I introduce Stick Dog's four friends, I know what you are going to say. You're going to say, "Hey. These four friends

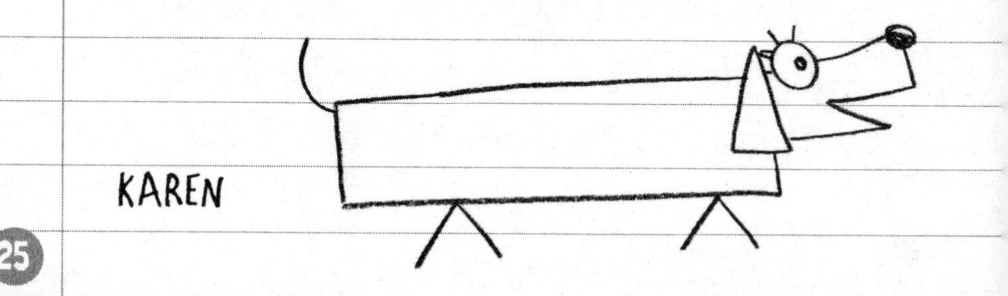

look remarkably similar to the four types of other dogs in the last chapter." You're absolutely right about that. But they're the only kinds of dogs I can draw. And please remember our deal.

Stick Dog has four friends who stop by his empty pipe on a regular basis. There's a poodle named Poo-Poo. Now, it's important to know that Poo-Poo is not named after, you know, going to the bathroom. He's named after his own name. Get it? POO-dle.

There's also a Dalmatian named Stripes. Stripes likes to be a little oddballish. She's covered in spots, but her name is Stripes. See what I mean? If she was, say, all black from nose to tail, then her name would probably be Snowball. Stripes is the kind of dog who would look at a gray, rainy day and say something like "Let's go on a picnic!" or "What a great day for a bike ride!" Of course, dogs don't typically ride bikes—but you get what I mean.

Then there's a dachshund. Her name is Karen. This is kind of a human name, but it's her name, and there's not much we can do about it. It's kind of like if your uncle was named Snoopy. You wouldn't call him Uncle Bob. You'd call him Uncle Snoopy. Of course, if your buddies were around and you didn't want them to know that your uncle's name was Snoopy, you might just call him Uncle Man or Unc-Dude or Unc-a-Munc-a-Ding-Dong or something.

Anyway, this dachshund's name is Karen.

There's also a dog named Mutt. He's a mutt. Enough said.

Chapter 3
A PLEASANT AROMA IS DETECTED

Stick Dog has a nice home and good friends.

But when it comes to being a dog, there's something else that's really super-important. I bet you can guess what that is. If you're a dog, you can almost certainly guess what it is.

Then again, if you're a dog and you're reading this story, then you should probably stop reading right now. You may not know this, but dogs that can read are extremely rare. And that means you have the opportunity to be rich and famous and have all the rawhide bones and puppy snicker-snacks in the world. So get yourself down to the local television station and start reading in front of everybody.

Now, if you're not a dog reading this story, I'm going to assume that you are a human. If you are, then try to guess what's just as important (maybe even more important) to a dog than a safe home and good friends.

Give up?

The answer is food. Food, food, food, food, FOOD.

Don't be embarrassed if you didn't guess right. One time my first-grade teacher asked me what holiday happens at the end of November. And I said, "Pumpkin pie!"

What? I like pumpkin pie. So sue me.

My point is, don't feel bad if you didn't guess that FOOD was the answer. It happens. It's no big deal. That said, if you did guess that FOOD was the answer, it doesn't exactly make you the next Mega-genius of the World or anything. It's a pretty obvious answer—even if you're not a dog.

Anyway, Stick Dog and his friends are constantly in search of food. And that's what this adventure is all about.

This story takes place in the summer. And when you live in the suburbs and it's the summer, it can mean only one thing. (Actually, it can mean a lot of things, like: *It's time to cut the grass* or *Let's go play in the sprinkler* or *If another mosquito bites me, I'm going to be all out of blood.*)

But for Stick Dog, summer in the suburbs

means humans are grilling out. And when humans are grilling out, the air is filled with the aroma of tasty, sizzling hamburgers. And tasty, sizzling hamburgers are about the best things in the world to Stick Dog.

On this particular afternoon, all of Stick Dog's buddies—Poo-Poo, Mutt, Stripes, and, of course, Karen—have stopped by. And because the wind is blowing at seven miles per hour from the southwest, the grill aromas from Picasso Park are drifting right past the empty pipe beneath Highway 16.

And Stick Dog has caught the scent. He's got to get a hamburger.

Now, there are two things that can happen as I tell you this story. I can use dog language; you know: yips, yaps, barks—that kind of thing. Or I can interpret all of the dog language for you.

This translation will work for all human readers. And if you're a dog reader, you really should be at the television station by now.

So, here goes.

"I've got to get a hamburger," Stick Dog said, his stomach rumbling a bit as the meaty smoke wafted past his nose.

"How?" asked Poo-Poo.

"We're going to need a plan," Mutt added. "Humans aren't just going to *give* us hamburgers."

"Certainly not. They're selfish. They want to keep all the hamburgers for themselves." Stick Dog shook his head in disgust, muttering under his sweet-smelling dog breath about how humans never share anything. He rose off the couch cushion and, shaking the dirt from his fur, said, "Let's follow the smell, find the hamburgers. Find the hamburgers, make a plan. Execute the plan, eat the hamburgers."

"Eat the hamburgers," Stripes added, "roll around in the dirt scratching our backs."

"Umm, yeah. Whatever," said Karen, scrunching up her face.

All of them trailed Stick Dog, who followed the scent toward Picasso Park. But as they went in search of some smoky hamburger goodness, their mission was interrupted by something very bad. Something was lurking in the Forest.

Chapter 4
AN ACORN DROPS IN THE FOREST

With Stick Dog in the lead, all five dogs sprinted off in search of yummy hamburgers. Twenty paws charging across the twigs, leaves, and sticks of the forest floor created a thunderous racket. But it was a thunderous racket only for a couple of minutes. Then something happened.

Poo-Poo saw a squirrel.

"STOP! Everybody stop!" yelled Poo-Poo as he skidded to a halt.

Karen, Stripes, and Mutt stopped quickly beside Poo-Poo. "What?" they asked.

"Up there!" Poo-Poo exclaimed, and lifted his nose up in the air to point. "Squirrel. In the oak tree!"

The four dogs gathered around the trunk of the tree. Stick Dog stood off to the side. The smell of those hamburgers was even stronger now.

"Hey, you guys," said Stick Dog. "Let's keep going and track down those hamburgers.

I'm starting to get pretty hungry."

Poo-Poo snapped his head toward Stick Dog and looked him in the eye. "You must not have heard me," he said. "There's a squirrel up there."

He turned back to the tree.

Stick Dog knew this delay would only make his hunger worse. He said, "I heard you, Poo-Poo. And I know how important squirrels are to you. I really do. It's just that—"

"They're more than just important to me," said Poo-Poo. "That's a gross underexaggeration. Squirrels are my archenemies! Ever since I was a puppy on the dairy farm, they've been torturing me."

"You grew up on a dairy farm, Poo-Poo?" Mutt asked.

"I think so. I remember there were cows everywhere," he answered, never once taking his eyes off his enemy in the tree. "And there were squirrels everywhere too. With their sniffy little noses and their chattering sounds. And then those puffy tails. Oooh, I can't stand those puffy tails.

Like they're so great. 'Look at us! We have puffy tails. Aren't we so special?'"

Stick Dog came a step closer and glanced up into the oak tree. "Poo-Poo, I might not feel quite as strongly as you do about squirrels—"

"They're evil!" Poo-Poo interrupted. "Truly evil."

"Okay, okay. They're evil," said Stick Dog. "I just wonder why we have to worry about this *particular* squirrel in this *particular* tree at this *particular* time. We're on our way to find tasty hamburgers. With a good strategy and some good teamwork, we could be feasting on hamburgers in no time."

Poo-Poo was quiet and still. Stick Dog hoped that he was absorbing the words and would decide to abandon the squirrel—and continue their mission.

"Did you see that?!" Poo-Poo screamed. "It just twitched its tail at me. Arrgg! I can't stand it when they do that. That drives me crazy!"

"Could you just forget about it this one time?" Stick Dog asked.

Poo-Poo paused and considered. "Well, maybe . . ."

And then the squirrel dropped an acorn on Poo-Poo's head.

Poo-Poo jumped up, barking furiously, and put his front paws as high as he could on the trunk of the tree. "Why you rotten, little, furry, no-good, fuzzy-tailed, nut-eating, acorn-dropping, sneaky, tree-climbing beast!" he yelled.

"What happened?" asked Karen.

"You're not going to believe what that fuzzy gray trickster did to me!" exclaimed Poo-Poo.

"What? What did he do?" asked Mutt and Stripes.

"That puffy-tailed, nose-twitching, branch-jumping little scoundrel dropped an acorn on my head!"

"He didn't," said Karen. "I can't believe it."

"He did," Poo-Poo answered, his eyes fixed on the top branches of that tree.

"This is the last time," said Poo-Poo, now circling the tree and growling at the uppermost branches. "I've had it with their twitchy tails and their oh-so-superior

tree-jumping skills and fancy wire-walking expertise. And I've really had it with their acorn-dropping ways. It's time to set things right and restore the natural order of things. Dogs are better than squirrels—and today I'm going to prove it."

"How are you going to do that, Poo-Poo?" asked Karen.

"I'm not sure, but I'm thinking I'll just wait here until that squirrel comes down," said Poo-Poo. He stopped and brought a paw to his chin. "But that might be a while. That nasty, little, gray fluff ball probably has a stash of food up there somewhere. That would be just like a squirrel!"

"So what *are* you going to do?" asked Mutt.

"I'll just have to find a way up."

Now, I don't know if you know this or not, but dogs can't climb trees.

And this presented a dilemma.

Do you know what a dilemma is? It's when you have a choice among things to do, but none of the options is very good. Let's see; let me think of an example. Okay, here's one. It's dinnertime, and you have two vegetables to choose from: overcooked green beans or steamed cauliflower. And

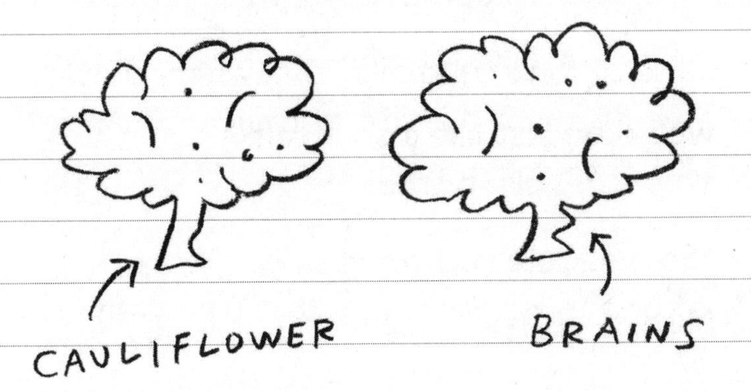

your mom says you have to pick one. You, my vegetable-avoiding friend, are now faced with a "dilemma."

Actually, I don't mind cauliflower that much. Except it kind of looks like brains. And, let's face it, that's not something you want to be thinking about when you're eating. I just ruined cauliflower for you, didn't I? Well, enjoy your overcooked green beans.

So Poo-Poo's dilemma was this: he could wait for that squirrel to come down, which could take forever—or he could find a way up, which is pretty tough for a dog who can't climb trees.

After a few laps around that tree with his

face contorted in deep thought, Poo-Poo stopped and stood before his four friends.

"Does anyone here have a huge rubber band?" he asked. "About six feet long and really, really stretchy?"

Stick Dog shook his head. So did Karen and Stripes.

"Fresh out," answered Mutt.

"Why do you want one?" asked Karen.

"Well, with all the trees around here, I thought I could string a giant rubber band between a couple of trunks to create a slingshot. Then I could shoot my way up there to get that whisker-twitching menace to society."

Mutt, Karen, and Stripes nodded in understanding. Stick Dog didn't say anything.

"How about a cannon? Anybody have a cannon?" Poo-Poo asked. "Same principle as the slingshot, just a different kind of shooting mechanism. Anybody?"

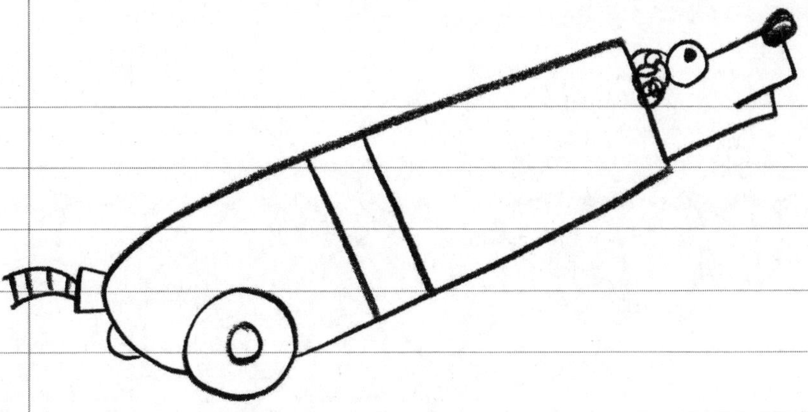

Stick Dog, Karen, and Stripes shook their heads again.

"Not with me," replied Mutt.

"Dang it," Poo-Poo said. He began to tap his left forepaw against the ground in rapid taps. He was thinking hard—very hard. "I got it, I got it. Somebody here has to have a trampoline, right? You know those big contraptions with the springs around the outside and a big, rubbery circle thing in the middle? I've seen humans jumping real

high on those things. Do any of you have one of those? Anyone? Anyone?"

Stick Dog said he didn't. Stripes and Karen did the same.

Mutt splayed his legs and shook his whole body as if he thought there was a chance a trampoline might fall out of his fur. He studied the ground beneath him and seemed disappointed to find there was no trampoline. "Not today," he answered.

"This is great, just great," Poo-Poo moaned. "Here I have this devious, conniving chatterbox practically within my grasp, and I can't finish the job."

Finally Stick Dog rose to his feet. He knew the squirrel was not practically within

Poo-Poo's grasp at all. But he also knew they had to get to the park as fast as possible if they wanted any chance at a hamburger feast. Every minute of delay meant their hunger would grow more severe. It also meant the hamburgers might be eaten before they even had a chance to grab them. Stick Dog knew he had to act.

He came to the tree, stood shoulder to shoulder with Poo-Poo, and whispered to him, "I see what you mean now. That acorn dropping on your head made it all too clear. It's time to deal with this tail-twitcher."

Poo-Poo, clearly surprised, turned his head and stared at Stick Dog.

"Poo-Poo's right!" Stick Dog shouted up in the general direction of the squirrel. He couldn't really see it, but that didn't really matter to him. "I've had it with sniveling, tail-shaking chatter-mouths like you!"

Mutt, Karen, and Stripes all stared at Stick Dog too, curiosity and surprise on their faces.

"We can wait all week if we have to. No food, no water—no problem." Stick Dog was doing his best to look as tough as he could. He squinted his eyes and tried to snarl. It was not something he was very good at. "Do you smell that hamburger aroma coming from the park, you fuzzy tail-shaker? Do you!?"

The squirrel was paying no attention. It was digging the nut out from an acorn shell. The dogs, however, had rediscovered the scent of hamburger. Their noses were lifted in the air.

"See how good that smells?" Stick Dog continued shouting. "Well, we don't care one bit. Those humans can cook a million tasty hamburgers and eat them all! So what if we don't get any?!"

"Uhh, Stick Dog?" Mutt whispered. There was a look of concern on his face.

"If we have to wait until we're just skin and bones and grilling season is over and we never eat again, that's fine by us!" Stick Dog continued.

"Stick Dog, could I have a word?" asked Karen. She appeared bothered as well.

Stick Dog pretended not to hear her. He shouted, "Hey, you up there! I want you to know that I agree one hundred percent with Poo-Poo. I'll gladly sacrifice a chance at delicious, juicy hamburgers. So what if we haven't had anything to eat since yesterday morning! So what if we never get another chance like this again?"

"Excuse me? Umm, Stick Dog?" said Stripes.

But Stick Dog went on. "I know that meaty juice and smoky flavor will be the best we ever tasted. And it would be so nice to have warm food for a change. We almost always find cold food. We never get warm food like hamburgers from the grill. But it doesn't matter! We're not going anywhere!"

"Stick Dog?" Poo-Poo tried to interrupt.

But Stick Dog kept going. "Just to show you how committed I am, I'm going to take a big sniff of the air and NOT leave. Are you watching?"

Stick Dog took a huge sniff of the air, and as he suspected they would, the other dogs did too. The wind was drifting in the perfect direction, blowing the mouth-watering, hamburger-scented breeze right to them. He heard the slow, deep rumble of the other dogs' stomachs. From the corner of his eye, he saw Poo-Poo close his eyes and lick his lips.

"Doesn't that smell extra delicious, Mr. Twitchy-Pants?" Stick Dog called to the squirrel. "I can almost taste them. We don't care though. We're not leaving! No way!"

"Hey, uhh, Stick Dog?"

"Yes, Poo-Poo," Stick Dog answered, not lowering his head yet.

"I'm thinking," Poo-Poo said, "that maybe we should go get those hamburgers and worry about proving our superiority to squirrels later."

"Are you sure?"

"Stick Dog," Poo-Poo declared, "I've never been so sure of anything in my life."

Stick Dog lowered his head and stretched his legs, preparing for the rest of the journey to Picasso Park. "If you're sure that's what you want to do, Poo-Poo."

Poo-Poo nodded quickly and wagged his tail. "What are we waiting for? Let's go!" Without even looking up, Poo-Poo ran

right past the oak tree—and the squirrel that was in it.

Stick Dog smiled. "To the park," he said to Mutt, Stripes, and Karen.

And off they ran.

Chapter 5
A WARRIOR-HUMAN ATTACKS

It was about a two-mile run to the park. They traveled across a creek, up and down several tree-covered hills, and across a meadow. Picasso Park was surrounded by walnut trees, goldenrod clumps, cattail reeds, and honeysuckle bushes.

The dogs settled in behind some of the shrubbery, safely out of sight of any humans.

Mutt inhaled deeply, taking in the aromas from the grill on the other side of Picasso

HAMBURGERVILLE

Park. "Welcome to Hamburgerville," he said with a grin. "Population: Us."

Karen groaned and rolled her eyes.

"Follow me," said Stick Dog. "We need to be able to see a little better."

They flattened themselves against the ground and scurried forward on their bellies, pulling themselves with their front legs. Several small hills surrounded the park, and it was atop one of these hills where the dogs stopped beneath a walnut tree. All five dogs peered toward a gazebo on the other side of Picasso Park.

A woman with a yellow apron was grilling. Two kids, a boy and a girl, were kicking a soccer ball back and forth. And a man, presumably the father, was setting out paper plates on a picnic table.

"This is going to be tougher than I thought," said Stick Dog, peeking over the top of the hill. "There are four humans. That's more than I'd hoped. I thought we could all run in as fast as possible—"

Stick Dog stopped talking. He didn't stop talking because he had finished his thought. He stopped talking because Stripes had suddenly sprinted down the hill as fast as she could toward the smoking barbecue grill.

"Where's she going?!" asked Stick Dog.

"I think she heard you say 'run in as fast

as possible' and, uhh—" Mutt lost his train of thought as he watched Stripes fly down that hill at full speed. She was a streaking black-and-white blur. "And, uhh, she, like, took off."

"I hadn't finished my sentence," said Stick Dog, exasperated. "I was going to say I thought we could all run in as fast as possible and grab the hamburgers, but we *won't be able to* now because there are too many humans. If there was just one, or even two, maybe we could have handled it. But not four. We need to come up with something clever."

"Stick Dog?" Poo-Poo asked.

"Yes." Stick Dog sighed. He was frustrated that Stripes had zoomed off, and he hoped Poo-Poo might have a solution.

Poo-Poo was looking up into the walnut tree nervously. "Could we move out from under this tree? These are really big nuts.

If there's a nasty, tail-shaking squirrel up there and he drops one of these walnut-bombs on my head, it's really going to hurt."

Stick Dog closed his eyes for a moment. "Let's not worry about that right now,

Poo-Poo," he said. "We'll move in a minute. I promise. Right now we have to worry about Stripes running off by herself against four humans."

"Look! She's almost there!" Karen exclaimed.

"Man, she's fast!" said Mutt.

"I've seen faster," said Poo-Poo, unimpressed. "She's going downhill, and the wind's behind her, that's all."

Stripes was indeed almost there. She had begun to slow her pace and shorten her stride as she approached the unattended grill. None of the family had seen her yet. The boy and the girl were off in the grass on the other side of the gazebo, while the man and the woman were unpacking supplies from a wicker basket.

Stripes slowed to a walk and then stopped. She hid behind a bench near the grill. It was only then that she looked around and realized she was alone. Her head jerked up and her eyes focused on Stick Dog, Mutt, Karen, and Poo-Poo, who were staring at her from the top of the hill.

It was at this exact moment—when Stripes was looking away from the gazebo—that the mother unpacked a long, silver, two-pronged fork.

When Stripes turned back around, there

was the mother holding that long, silver, two-pronged fork. It glinted and shone in the sunlight as she carried it toward the grill.

That was all Stripes needed to see. Any thought of trying to grab those hamburgers by herself vanished. She stared at the woman through the back slats of the bench. The woman came nearer, holding that fork, then snapped her fingers and turned around, returning to the basket.

That was the split-second opportunity Stripes needed. She came sprinting back up to the top of the hill.

"Get down! Get down!" Stick Dog said

urgently to the others. "We can't let them see us!"

They all scooched back, out of sight of the family. It was only a matter of seconds before Stripes came hurtling over the top of the hill to join them.

"What happened? Where were you guys?!" she asked, panting.

"I hadn't finished talking," Stick Dog said. "I was saying, I wanted all of us to run in as fast as possible—"

"Yeah, yeah!" Stripes interrupted. "That's what I did!"

"—but we wouldn't be able to because there were too many people. You ran off before I could finish my sentence," Stick Dog explained.

"Oh," Stripes said, and dropped her head a little, still panting. "Sorry about that."

"Just stay here with us, okay?"

"Okay, sure thing," said Stripes. Her voice turned deadly serious as she addressed

Poo-Poo, Karen, and Mutt. "Listen, I've got very bad news. Those aren't just normal humans down there. They're like super-warrior humans or something. Very mean and very dangerous, I think. They have weapons."

"What do you mean?" asked Mutt.

"That warrior-woman," Stripes said, "has a double-bladed silver sword."

"That was a big fork," Stick Dog said, but nobody heard him. The others were focused on Stripes. The fear and anxiety in her voice commanded all of their attention.

"She was charging at me!"

"She was walking," Stick Dog corrected.

"She was going to stab me with it!"

"She was going to flip the hamburgers on the grill."

"Then she went back to that evil basket to get another weapon."

"She was getting salt." Stick Dog sighed again.

Mutt, Poo-Poo, and Karen didn't hear anything that Stick Dog had said. They were starting to panic. Their fear made them back farther and farther down the hill, away from the park. And to Stick Dog's dismay, away from the hamburgers.

"Stop," Stick Dog said firmly. "Everyone calm down. Come back up here. They're not warriors with weapons. They're just having a picnic, and they use that metal thing to cook the hamburgers. That's all."

"They don't use it to stab hamburger thieves?" asked Stripes.

"Of course not," Stick Dog said.

"Are you sure?" Mutt, Karen, and Poo-Poo asked in unison, inching back up the slope toward Stick Dog.

"I'm sure." Stick Dog nodded. "Come on. Come look."

They all peered down at the gazebo. Sure enough, the woman was turning the hamburgers with the long silver fork.

"I don't know, Stick Dog," Mutt said, still wary. "This might be too dangerous. Look at the two little humans. They look like warriors too."

"How so?"

"Well, that girl can kick that black-and-white ball about a hundred miles per hour. And that boy—just look at him! He's letting the ball hit him right on top of the head over and over again."

"That's amazing!" said Karen.

"I'm pretty sure that's just how they play with that kind of ball," said Stick Dog.

"Are you nuts?" Mutt exclaimed. "What kind of creature would let himself get knocked on the head over and over like that?!"

"Stick Dog?" asked Poo-Poo, looking back up at the walnut tree.

"Yes?" Stick Dog answered, trying to keep his composure. His stomach now felt almost empty. And the smell of those sizzling hamburgers was drifting right up the hill at them.

"Can we *please* move out from under this tree?"

"Yes, yes," said Stick Dog. "Follow me—nice and low—to that honeysuckle bush."

They all followed Stick Dog to the honeysuckle bush. Something about the sweet aroma of the honeysuckle flowers and Stick Dog's soothing voice settled the other four dogs considerably.

"All right. Time to make a plan," said Stick Dog. "We've made it this far. We've *found* the hamburgers. Now we just have to figure out how to *get* the hamburgers."

Chapter 6

KAREN IS MISSING

"I've got an idea," Mutt said.

"Great," said Stick Dog. "What's your plan?"

"There are four of them and five of us," Mutt began. "So me, Stripes, Karen, and Poo-Poo each choose a person."

Mutt turned and pointed toward Stripes and Poo-Poo with his nose. Then he swiveled his head to the left and right a few times. He asked, "Where's Karen?"

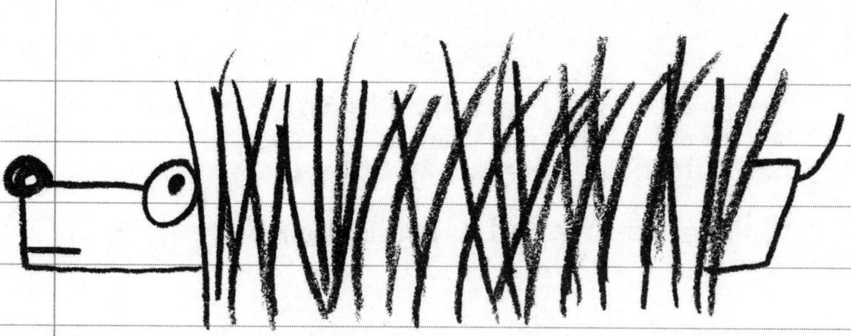

Now, Karen, of course, is a dachshund. The top of her head is only about eight inches tall, and the top of her back is only about five inches off the ground. Stripes, Poo-Poo, Mutt, and Stick Dog had lost Karen before. Once when the lawnmower man at Picasso Park was on vacation, they had lost Karen in a patch of very thick, very tall grass.

So there was no need to be alarmed.

Yet.

To avoid being overheard by the hamburger-grilling family, Stick Dog whispered low and hard, "Karen. Karen!"

Do you know what whispering "low and hard" means? It's the kind of whisper my mom uses when she discovers I'm chewing Bubble Yum bubble gum in the library. My favorite flavor? Original. Even though "original" is not technically a flavor, if you think about it.

Karen didn't answer.

"She must be in the brush somewhere," said Stick Dog, his stomach rumbling loudly. "Help me look around, please—quietly."

The four of them spread out and began using my mom's you're-so-busted-chewing-Bubble-Yum-original-flavor-bubble-gum-in-the-library whisper.

"Karen! Karen!"

Stripes searched through some cattail reeds. Mutt pawed through a bunch of leaves that the wind had blown into a pile. Poo-Poo stood on his hind legs and looked up into the top branches of a sycamore tree.

Stick Dog called them back together.

"Anything?"

They all shook their heads.

"This is awful," moaned Mutt. "What could have happened to her?"

"She was here just a minute ago," said Poo-Poo.

"I'm really going to miss her," said Stripes. "I'm going to miss watching her chase her tail and not catch it. I'll miss watching her try to jump high off the ground even though her legs can only push her about two inches in the air. She really was entertaining, you know. What a loss."

"And that tail," said Poo-Poo, dropping his head and staring at the ground. "Whenever she was happy, that tail could really get wagging. I remember once, I was too close to her when she found half of a potato chip by her favorite garbage can at Picasso Park. . . ."

Stick Dog turned to look toward Karen's favorite garbage can.

"She loved potato chips," Mutt added.

"I know she did," continued Poo-Poo, nodding his head at the memory. "I was right next to her when she found that chip. Her favorite chip-finding place had paid off again. Remember how she always went there first whenever we went to the park? That garbage can next to the basketball court? Well, she found a chip that time, and her tail started swishing like crazy and whacked me three times right across the face. Smack! Smack! Smack! Good old Karen. I'll really miss her dangerous tail-wagging ways."

Mutt nodded his head.

"It's a terrible tragedy, all right," sighed Mutt. He stared up at a lone gray cloud in the sky as it drifted in front of the sun. "I think maybe when we get those juicy, warm hamburgers from the humans, we should leave one in her memory at Karen's favorite location."

"Where's that?" asked Stick Dog.

"It's where Poo-Poo said: Karen's favorite garbage can," said Mutt. "She went there every time we went to the park. Don't you remember? It was always the first place she sprinted off to whenever we got near the place. Jeez, Stick Dog, I can't believe you don't remember. It's as if the memory of Karen is already slipping away from you."

Stick Dog looked across the park again. "Right, I remember now," he said, smiling to himself.

Mutt blinked quickly a couple of times. "I just think a hamburger would be a good memorial to her."

There was complete silence for several moments. It was difficult to tell what Stripes and Poo-Poo were thinking about Mutt's idea.

"Let me get this straight," Poo-Poo finally said in a low, shaky voice. "You think we should go to all this trouble—even risk getting caught—to get those hamburgers

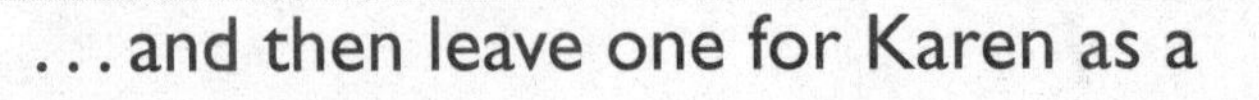
. . . and then leave one for Karen as a memorial?"

"That's right," said Mutt. The sun had begun to emerge from the other side of that single dark cloud in the sky. "As a way to honor and remember her."

"Umm," said Poo-Poo. He stopped and

took a deep breath. "It's a nice idea and all. But I'm not risking my life and four limbs to get a hamburger that we're not even going to eat. Forget it. With my luck, some tail-shaking, chattering squirrel would find it and eat it. I miss Karen and all, but let's try to stay serious here."

"You don't think we should do something to honor Karen?" Mutt asked, beginning to sound offended.

"Not with hamburgers," Poo-Poo

answered. "They're too precious. Can't we all come here and howl on her birthday or something?"

Stick Dog was willing to let this conversation go on—but his stomach was not. It was growling even louder than before. And as you can probably guess,

Stick Dog had found Karen by this time. She was, in fact, right in the spot they were describing: at the garbage can next to the basketball court.

"Where is her favorite garbage can again, Mutt?" Stick Dog asked.

"It's right over there," he began, finally looking away from the sky. The dark gray

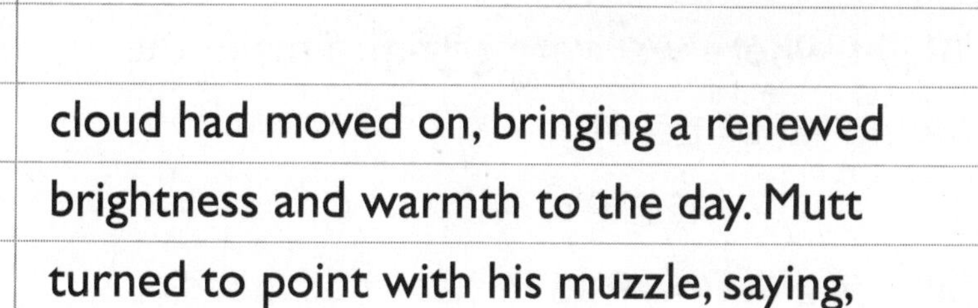

cloud had moved on, bringing a renewed brightness and warmth to the day. Mutt turned to point with his muzzle, saying,

"The garbage can next to the bask—"

Mutt stopped talking suddenly, and his tail started swishing faster and faster. His eyes opened wide. "I found her!"

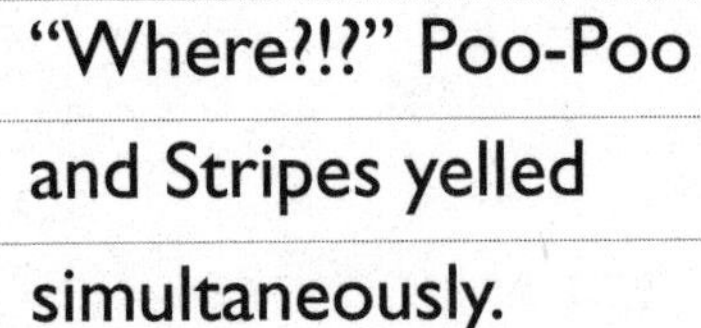

"Where?!?" Poo-Poo and Stripes yelled simultaneously.

"There!" Mutt screamed. It was difficult to tell where he was pointing though. He was leaping up and down and shaking with excitement. "Right where we were going to make the memorial to her!"

Stripes and Poo-Poo jerked their heads

around to look. Sure enough, there was Karen. They all began hopping up and down in place with their tails wagging like mad and whipping into one another.

Stick Dog was, of course, happy to find Karen too. But he had known for a little while where she was and that she was safe.

Karen was digging around in some loose trash that had blown out of the garbage can. That's why she loved this particular one. It filled up quickly because a lot of small humans played on the basketball court and a lot of older, larger humans watched them, eating snacks as they did.

This trash can, Karen knew, was also far away from the Dumpster. And that meant that the big humans who rode the giant blue truck and collected garbage on Thursday mornings often didn't fetch this can—especially if it was raining. And Karen knew that this very full garbage can often overflowed. She knew a brisk wind could pick up a loose potato chip bag and blow it off the top—leaving tasty, salty morsels inside for her to find with her skinny, perfectly proportioned dachshund muzzle.

And that's just what had happened—and just what she had found. Karen had a small, bright orange bag covering her nose. And she was trying to return to her four friends behind the honeysuckle bush.

"Here she comes!" yelled Poo-Poo.

"That's her all right!" screamed Stripes.

Mutt laughed and shook his head. "Good old Karen."

Now, a dachshund running across a field with a bag on its head is quite a sight to see. It also takes a long time to see it. Dachshunds are not really that fast. Sure, they can move along pretty well, but three-inch legs can only cover so much ground no matter how fast they're churning. And when a dachshund has her head in a potato chip bag, that tends to slow things down considerably.

Another problem? The bag was large enough to ride up over Karen's eyes as well. So the combination of short legs, a bag on her head, and a lack of vision made for a lengthy zigzaggy trip to the other four dogs behind the honeysuckle bush.

But at last she reached them, dropped

the bag, picked it up by the bottom, and poured out the contents. "I love that garbage can! Look at all these!" she exclaimed. "I brought them back to share. You know, as an appetizer before our hamburgers. Appetizers are really important. I learned that when I lived in the back of that restaurant for a while. The chef was always saying, 'A fine appetizer is the only way to start a fine meal.'"

MOUND OF CHIPS

"You lived in the back of a restaurant?" asked Stripes. "What kind of restaurant was it?"

"It was French-Asian fusion. Very trendy."

"You must have gotten great scraps."

Karen nodded her head. "Boy, did I. The French really know their sauces."

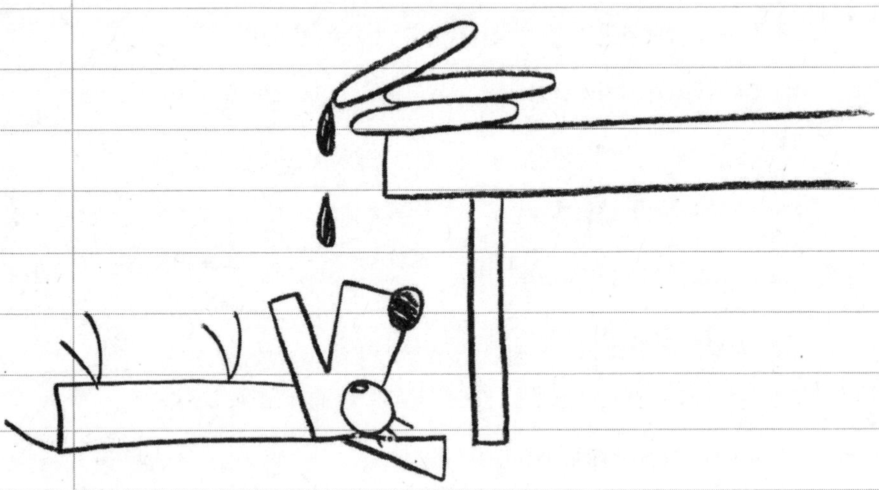

"Why in the world did you leave?"

"Well, they found out I was there after a couple of weeks." Karen smiled. "It was good eating for a while though. Anyway, that's where I learned about appetizers. I think chips make a great prequel to a big meal like hamburgers. That's why I went to my garbage can. There's almost always something to eat there."

The dogs all turned their attention back to the appetizer Karen had provided. There was a small mound of chips, perhaps ten in all, and plenty of crumbs.

"We're really glad you're back," said Stripes.

"Yeah," Poo-Poo added, leaning down to sniff the small pile of chips. "We thought we'd lost you."

Mutt came closer to the chips too. "And Poo-Poo wanted to eat your memorial hamburger."

Karen tilted her head and turned to Stick Dog for an explanation. This is what usually happened whenever it was hard for one of them to figure something out.

"Never mind," he said. "Tell us about these chips. They look different than usual."

Karen wagged her tail. "That's because these are not your usual, run-of-the-mill potato chips."

"They have red-and-gold powdery stuff on them," Stripes said. She had dropped down to eye the small pile of chips closely. "I don't know about these. They don't smell like regular potato chips to me."

Poo-Poo was braver. He picked up one of the small stray crumbs. He nibbled it at the very front of his mouth, rolled it a little bit back and forth on his tongue, and then swallowed very slowly and deliberately, closing his eyes as the tiny morsel went down his throat.

Stick Dog and the others watched this with great interest. They wanted to know if this new kind of potato chip was any good. They also found this slow, deliberate eating style very strange.

At last, Poo-Poo opened his eyes. With great sophistication and authority, he declared, "I must say, this powdery combination of spice and flavor is both enchanting and invigorating." He closed his eyes and licked his lips. Then he nodded his head, opened his eyes, looked slightly above the other dogs, and stated, "It achieves a delicate balance of taste and texture. I get hints of salt and pepper, yes. But also brown sugar, garlic, and tomato. These flavors work in perfect conjunction with the crunchy satisfaction of a good, crisp bite."

Karen, Mutt, Stripes, and Stick Dog stared at Poo-Poo. After a moment, he dropped his gaze to look at them.

"What?" he asked. "I happen to have very refined taste."

"I have to admit, Poo-Poo," said Stick Dog. "That's a very detailed description of those flavors. I can almost taste them myself. You really do have a talent for this kind of thing."

"Yes. Yes, I do," said Poo-Poo with a magnificent air of authority. "Once, a very long time ago, I was able to discern the difference between kibble and bits."

They ate two potato chips and several crumbs each, relishing this newfangled flavor for as long as they could.

"That was fantasti-melicious," Stripes said to Karen. "Thanks for providing that appetizer."

The other dogs expressed their gratitude to Karen as well. They licked their lips and the fur around their mouths, attempting to get every tiny morsel of flavor.

"Stick Dog?" asked Mutt. "How come I'm even hungrier than before? It doesn't make sense. After eating those chips, shouldn't I be more full? But my stomach feels more empty. That seems unfair."

This is a completely real feeling, by the way. You can test it at home. Wait for some time when you're superhungry. Then take one or two bites of something. Then wait a minute and don't eat anything else. You'll

often find that you've become super-duper extra hungry. I don't know why that is. I'm not a stomach doctor or anything. Kind of weird.

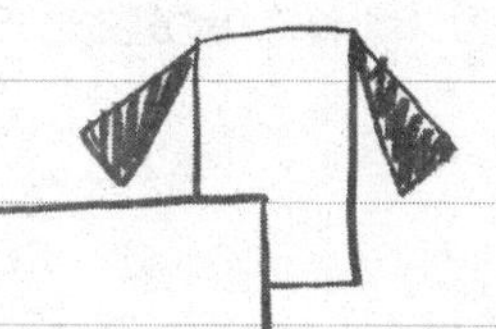

"I don't know why

that happens," answered Stick Dog. He was even hungrier than before too. "And I agree: it is completely unfair. It makes it even more vital for us to formulate a strategy and get those hamburgers."

All the dogs nodded in agreement.

"Mutt, you were about to tell us your plan," Stick Dog said, turning to him with a renewed sense of urgency in his voice. "What is it?"

Chapter 7
BITE, DRIVE, DIVE, AND FLY

"Well, I was thinking that there are four human creatures and five of us. So, the numbers work to our advantage," began Mutt. "Stripes, Poo-Poo, Karen, and I each choose a human. Then, on the count of three, we run across the field and bite the ankles of each human. While they're screaming in pain, Stick Dog grabs all the hamburgers off the grill and brings them back to his pipe for us to eat."

"Umm, okay," said Stick Dog. "That's one plan. Does anybody have a plan that doesn't involve biting people and me burning my paws off on a flaming barbecue grill?"

"You don't like my plan?" Mutt asked, a little depressed.

"Oh, that's not it at all," said Stick Dog. "It's a great plan. Let's just see if we can come up with an even greater plan."

This made Mutt feel better.

"I think I have an idea," Poo-Poo volunteered. "See that car over there? It must be theirs. It's the only one in the parking lot. What if I snatch the keys from the mom's bag? It's right there on the bench by the picnic table. Then I hop into the car and drive away. I won't steal it or anything. You know, just drive it a few blocks. The whole family of humans will chase me. While they're chasing me, you guys get the hamburgers and take them back to Stick Dog's pipe. Just save some for me, okay?"

Suddenly Mutt interrupted with a great deal of excitement. "Poo-Poo," he said, hopping up and down. "Can I ride in the passenger seat? And maybe roll down the window? I could stick my head out while you're driving. Is that okay? There's nothing like sticking your head out a window, man! All the different smells and sometimes you see other dogs on the sidewalk and you can bark your head off and there's wind in your ears and your fur. It's a blast. I mean, an absolute blast. Please let me! Please, please, PLEASE!"

"How do you know so much about riding in a car, Mutt?" asked Stripes.

"I used to go on my human's mail route

with him every Saturday. His name was Gary. He let me hang my head out the window."

"You lived with a *mailman*!?" asked Karen, shocked. "I bark at mailmen all the time. Maybe I barked at this Gary human."

"I doubt it," said Mutt, lowering his voice. "That was a long, long way from here."

"Will it bother you if we bark at mailmen? I mean, seeing as you used to have a human mailman of your own?"

Mutt shook his head and smiled. "Heck, no. In fact, I used to bark at Gary all the time."

"You did?" Poo-Poo asked. "You barked at your own human?"

"Umm, yeah. I'm a dog—and he was a mailman. What choice did I have?" Mutt said, clearly regarding this question as ridiculous. All of the other dogs agreed that this made perfectly good sense. Mutt returned to his original thought. "So, Poo-Poo, can I ride in the car during your most excellent plan?"

"Well," said Poo-Poo, "I was really planning on you helping with the hamburgers while I drive the car by myself."

"Come on, man," Mutt begged. It was obvious that he would do just about anything to ride in the car and hang his head out the window. His eyes popped open really wide. "I've got it! What if while I'm hanging out the window, I act as a lookout? I can tell you when the family is chasing us down, how close they're getting, if the police are after us, if you're about to run the car into a telephone pole—that kind of thing! That would be helpful, right? Wouldn't it? Wouldn't it?!"

"Well, let me think about it."

"I love riding in a car. It's the thing I miss the most. You have to take me," pleaded Mutt. "Sometimes you even get bugs in your teeth. And sometimes some of those bugs are delicious. I don't know which

ones because they fly into me at, like, thirty miles per hour and I can't see them. And because, you know, I swallow them. You just gotta let me come with you, Poo-Poo!"

"Well, okay," Poo-Poo finally responded.

"Yes!"

That's when Stick Dog spoke up. "One question, Poo-Poo," he said. "Do you know how to drive?"

Poo-Poo lowered his head. "No," he whispered. "Does that mess things up? Do you think it's a bad plan?"

"Not at all," said Stick Dog. "It's just such a good plan that I think we should save it for a very desperate time. Like when we're starving even more than today and must have some hamburgers. When that happens, we'll all say, 'Remember Poo-Poo's great plan from a couple of years ago? Let's use that.'"

"Oh, I see," said Poo-Poo. "Yes, that makes perfectly good sense."

"Good, I'm glad," said Stick Dog. "Anybody else?"

Mutt sat down and moaned to himself. "I really, really wanted to hang my head out of that car window," he mumbled. The other dogs felt sorry for him.

"If we get those hamburgers, Mutt," Stick Dog said, "I guarantee they'll taste better than the bugs that smash into your mouth when you ride in a car."

This thought lifted Mutt's mood immediately.

That's when Karen spoke up. She said, "I have a plan."

"Let's hear it," Stick Dog said.

Karen took a deep breath, her long dachshund abdomen inflating from front to back, and began. "It may hurt a little bit, but I think it's worth it," she said. "Let's go over to the creek and climb up that tall cliff right above that really shallow part. Then we jump off."

Karen stopped. Poo-Poo, Mutt, Stripes, and Stick Dog couldn't tell if that was the end of the plan or whether Karen was just taking another deep breath. Or perhaps whether she was contemplating how much it would hurt to fall off a cliff through about three inches of water—and land on a bunch of jagged rocks.

"Umm," said Stick Dog. "How does that get us any hamburgers?"

"Isn't it obvious?" Karen said, slightly put off.

"Well, yeah," answered Stick Dog. "But in a sort of nonobvious way. Maybe you could fill in some of the details for us."

"Oh, very well," said Karen. "After we jump off the cliff onto the rocks, we'll have lots of cuts and bruises, you see. Maybe even some broken bones! Won't that be wonderful?!"

"Yes, I suppose so," Stick Dog said slowly. "But, again, can we get to the getting-the-hamburgers part of the plan?"

Karen sighed the biggest, longest sigh a dachshund could sigh. Now, between you and me, that's not very big. Because, you know, dachshunds are not very big. But for Karen, it was as if she had sucked in enough air to fill up a blimp and then let it out again.

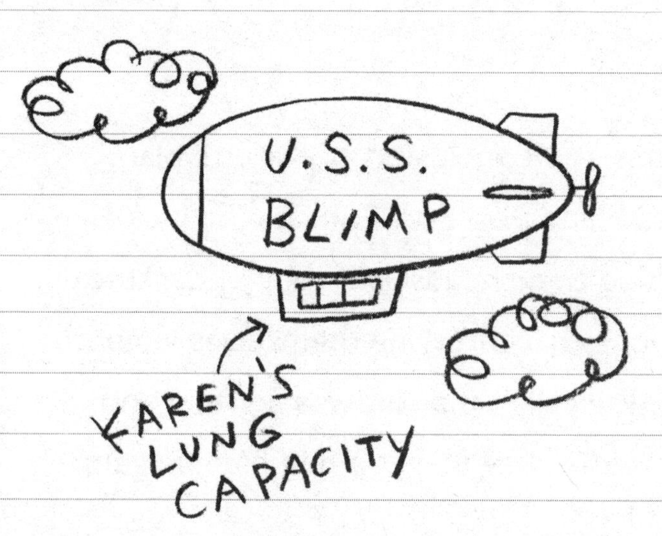

"We go up to the family," Karen explained. She spoke very slowly and seemed sort of embarrassed for her friends' lack of smarts. "And they give us the hamburgers because they feel sorry for us."

At this, the conclusion of Karen's plan, Mutt, Stick Dog, Poo-Poo, and Stripes all nodded their heads as if they understood all along that throwing themselves violently and tragically off a cliff was a grand and marvelous way to get a few hamburgers.

"Okay," said Stick Dog. "Let's call that Plan B."

"Plan B?" asked Karen incredulously. "Plan B?!?"

"Yes," said Stick Dog.

"Why?"

"Think about it. Plan B. *B*," Stick Dog explained, looking Karen right in the eyes. "*B* stands for 'Beautiful.' For 'Bountiful.' 'Bodacious.' 'Bombastic.'"

"'Brilliant'?" asked Karen quietly.

"Yes, of course," said Stick Dog. "'Brilliant' too."

At this, Karen puffed out her tiny dachshund chest with pride.

Stick Dog turned and looked at Stripes, who

was all too happy to offer a plan of her own.

"I see that, once again, it is up to my keen intellect and superior brain skills to devise a strategy for our success," said Stripes. "You will all listen carefully, please. I do not want to repeat this plan. A plan of this magnitude and brilliance is both effervescent and maxi-tastic."

"What is it?" Mutt sighed.

"It involves that big gazebo where the humans will eat their hamburgers," began Stripes. She paced back and forth in front of the other dogs. "I think we should put on a little show for the humans inside that gazebo. It will be like a theater play. We'll all act something out."

"Ooh, I love plays and acting!" screamed Poo-Poo.

"Good, I'm glad," continued Stripes. "We're going to act out a cops-and-robbers kind of play. With my background in law enforcement, I can lend real authenticity to the story."

"You used to be a police officer?" asked Mutt.

Stripes swelled with pride. "Well, sort of. I was a guard down at the mall." Stripes turned away for a moment and lowered her voice. "That all ended with the Nacho Cheese Grande incident."

"What Nacho Cheese Grande incident?"

"I don't want to talk about it," Stripes whispered, and her whole body shivered.

"Okay," said Stick Dog. He was anxious to get the hamburger-grabbing idea going again. He was so hungry now that his stomach was beginning to hurt a little. "Tell us more about the cops-and-robbers play that you're proposing."

Stripes hesitated for a few seconds more

to gather herself and then said, "First, Karen is going to run by the gazebo a couple of times with a really good-looking stick in her mouth. Second, Mutt and Poo-Poo come running up to the human family and turn their heads back and forth like they're looking for something. And they cry a lot."

"Why do we do that?" asked Mutt.

"You see, Karen has stolen the stick from you two," explained Stripes. "And you're very upset about it."

"Okay," said Stick Dog slowly. "What about you and me, Stripes?"

"Oh, we're on the roof," Stripes concluded. She headed toward the gazebo. "Come on, let's go. Follow me. Remember your parts."

Mutt, Poo-Poo, and Karen scurried out from behind the honeysuckle bush to follow Stripes.

"Wait a minute, wait a minute," said Stick Dog. "Come back here, please."

The other dogs stopped and came back.

"Why are you and I on the roof?" Stick Dog asked Stripes.

"Didn't I mention that part of the plan?" asked Stripes. "I apologize, Stick Dog. It just seemed so obvious that I didn't think it was worth mentioning. Allow me to explain."

"Please do," Stick Dog said.

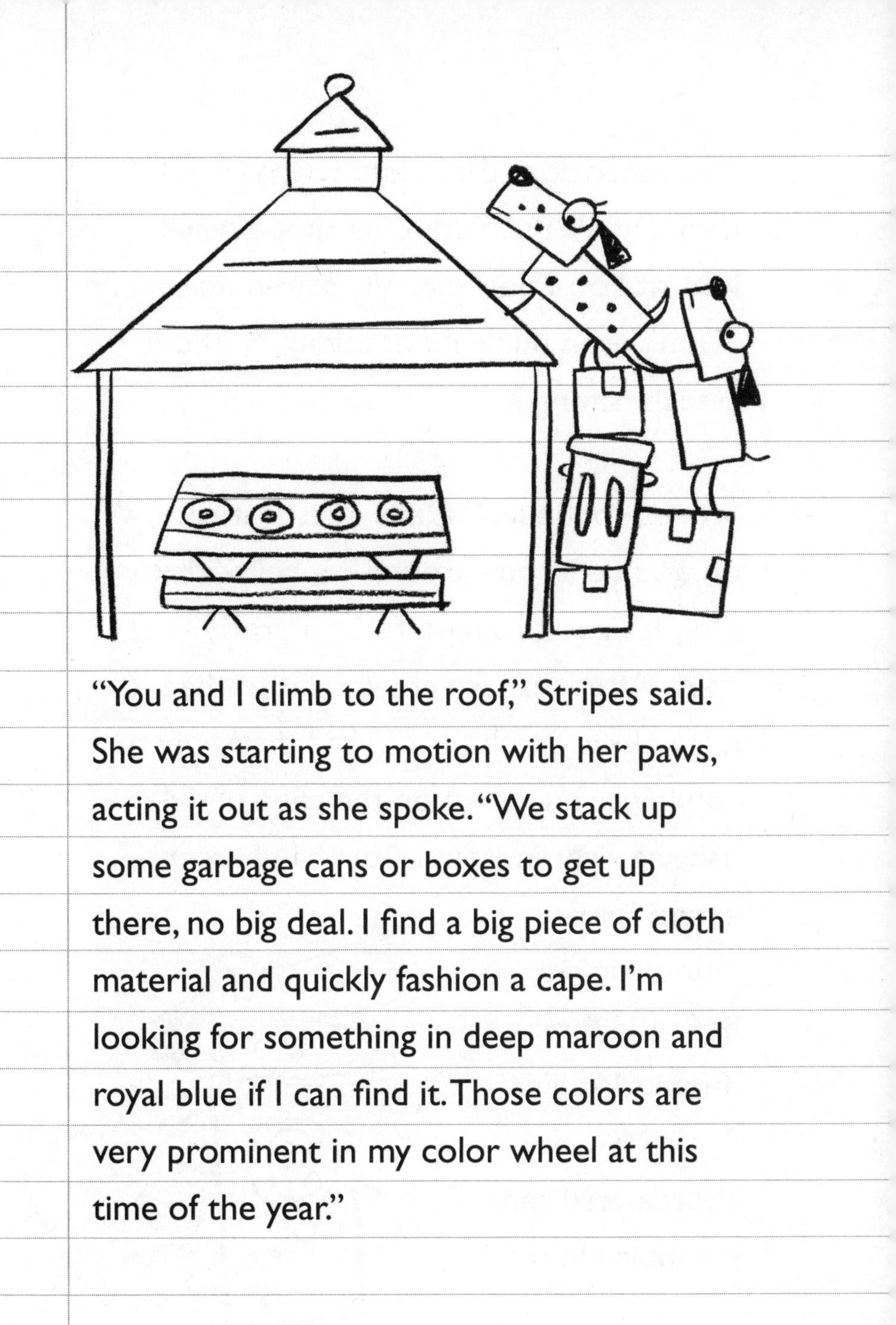

"You and I climb to the roof," Stripes said. She was starting to motion with her paws, acting it out as she spoke. "We stack up some garbage cans or boxes to get up there, no big deal. I find a big piece of cloth material and quickly fashion a cape. I'm looking for something in deep maroon and royal blue if I can find it. Those colors are very prominent in my color wheel at this time of the year."

The other dogs didn't know what this meant at all. But Stick Dog shot a quick look at Poo-Poo, Mutt, and Karen that said "Don't even think about asking" without actually saying it.

Stripes continued, "Once I get that cape on, you tie a rope around my belly, Stick Dog. It's going to have to be a pretty long rope. After that, we crawl right to the edge of the gazebo roof. And that's when you lower me down on the rope until I'm hanging right in front of the hamburger-eating humans. You swing me back and forth so it looks like I'm flying. My color-coordinated cape is flapping in the

wind behind me. It will look magnificent. And then—PRESTO!—hamburger time!"

Stick Dog inhaled very deeply. "Why are you wearing a cape?"

"I'm acting, remember? I'm Super-Dog!"

"You're Super-Dog?"

"I'm Super-Dog."

"And why are you swinging in the air?"

"Umm, to look like I'm flying," Stripes answered, and looked at the other dogs, nodding her head and smirking at Stick Dog.

"Of course. To look like you're flying," Stick Dog repeated. "And how does this great piece of theater get us the hamburgers?"

"In two ways. First, the family emerges from the gazebo to see Super-Dog save the day. Because, you know, how often do you get to see a flying dog chase down a stick-stealing criminal?"

"Not very often. Especially when Super-Dog is really just swinging back and forth from a rope," said Stick Dog.

"Right, exactly. And since they've run out of the gazebo, the hamburgers will be left unguarded," Stripes said. "By this time, Mutt, Poo-Poo, and Karen have run around the back of the gazebo out of sight. They can sneak in and snatch all of the hamburgers. While they're doing that, you swing me one more time, and I go bashing into the family, knocking them down and giving us even more time to complete our mission."

Stick Dog had no more questions, but Karen had one.

"Do I get to keep the stick?"

"Sure, no problem," answered Stripes.

"Well, it's a terrific plan," said Stick Dog. He knew there were actually quite a few flaws in Stripes's plan, including finding a cape and a rope, climbing to the top of the roof, and getting four humans to believe that a dog swinging back and forth from a rope was really a flying canine superhero and not, you know, a dog swinging back and forth from a rope.

But Stick Dog didn't mention any of these problems. He figured that if he could just take the blame quickly and simply, then maybe they could get to those hamburgers sooner. He said, "But I think I'm going to mess things up, Stripes. I'm just not strong enough to swing you back and forth like that. It's my fault your plan won't work. And I apologize for that."

Stripes looked very sad and dejected. She said, "It's okay, Stick Dog. I understand."

"It really is a good plan, Stripes," said Stick Dog.

Stripes still looked sad.

"Your spots look great today," he added. "They're really standing out nicely. The black spots combined with the white background are creating the perfect balance between lightness and darkness. And your fur looks especially clean and soft. Did you have a bath recently?"

"Yes, I did, as a matter of fact," said Stripes. "Just a few months ago."

"Well, we can certainly tell," said Stick Dog. "Right, everybody?"

“Yes. Mm-hmm. Oh, yeah,” Poo-Poo, Karen, and Mutt all chimed in quickly.

Stripes’s tail began wagging again. And when it did, she, Poo-Poo, Mutt, and Karen all gathered in a circle around Stick Dog. Because when it came to finding food, they knew Stick Dog would have a plan.

He always did.

Chapter 8

D-I-Z-T-R-A-K-S-H-U-N

"Yes, I have a plan," Stick Dog said before they could ask. "It involves creating a distraction. You all know what that is, right?"

They all nodded their heads, but Stick Dog wasn't convinced. In fact, after hearing their plans about throwing themselves off a cliff, biting people, swinging from a rope as Super-Dog, and driving away in the family's car, he was not confident at all that his four friends knew what a distraction was.

"Okay, then," Stick Dog said. "Mutt, what is a distraction?"

"A small bird from southeastern Australia known for its purple-and-gold plumage."

"No," Stick Dog said. "Poo-Poo, what is a distraction?"

"It's when you don't want to do anything except lie around," Poo-Poo answered.

"You're thinking of 'inaction,'" said Stick Dog. "Stripes, how about you?"

"Of course I know what it is," said Stripes with complete confidence. "'Distraction.' *D-I-Z-T-R-A-K-S-H-U-N.* 'Distraction.'"

"That's how you spell it. Actually that's *not*

how you spell it. But I wasn't asking for a spelling—or a misspelling—anyway. I was looking for a definition. A meaning."

"That I do not know," said Stripes with a great deal of pride for some reason.

Thankfully for Stick Dog, there was only one friend who had not answered yet. It was Karen. She said, "A distraction is when you combine two words with an apostrophe."

"You're thinking of a contraction." Stick Dog paused for a moment and then added, "And while that is not the correct definition of 'distraction,' I do have to tell you that I'm a little impressed that you know the definition of 'contraction.'"

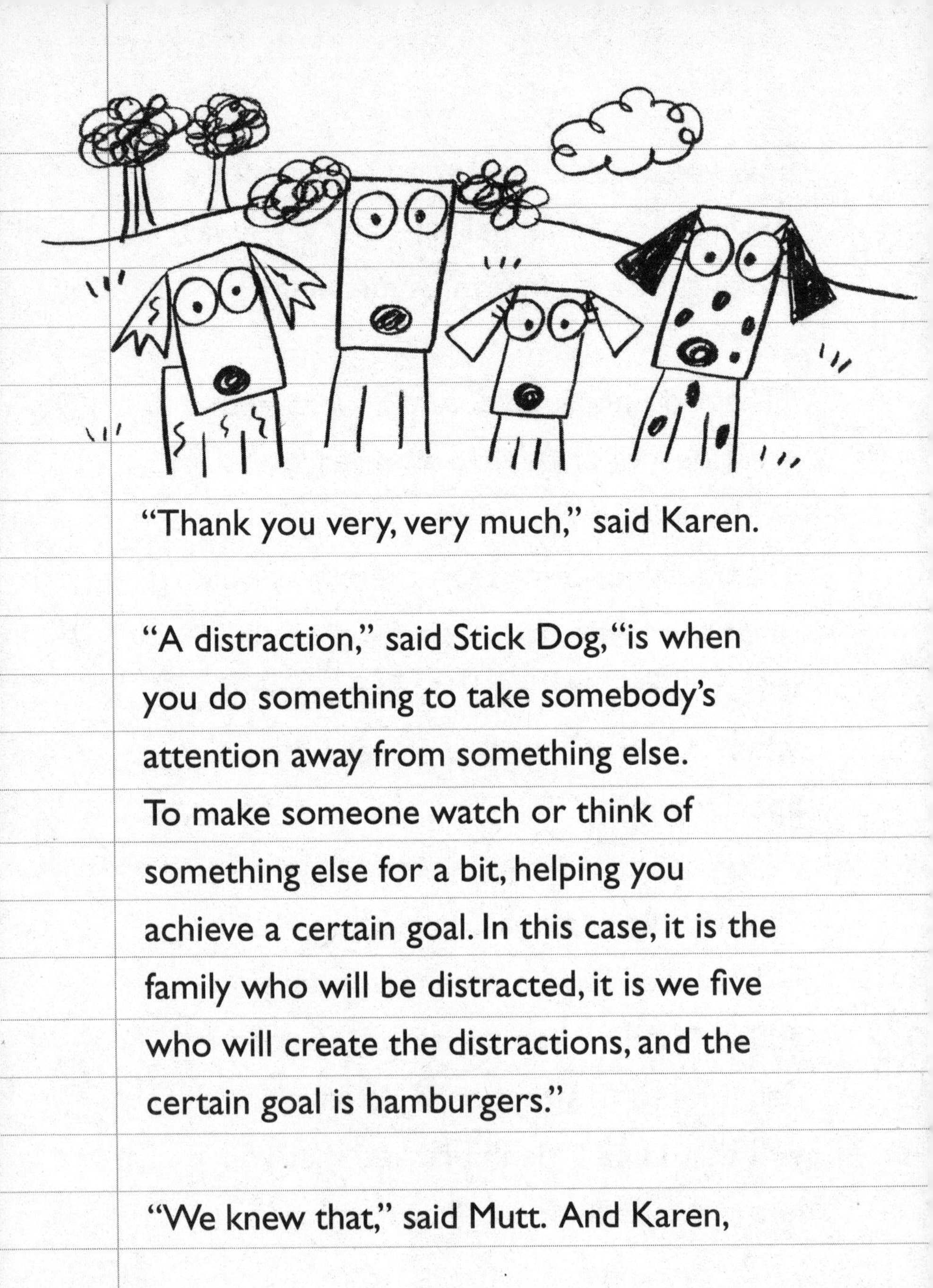

"Thank you very, very much," said Karen.

"A distraction," said Stick Dog, "is when you do something to take somebody's attention away from something else. To make someone watch or think of something else for a bit, helping you achieve a certain goal. In this case, it is the family who will be distracted, it is we five who will create the distractions, and the certain goal is hamburgers."

"We knew that," said Mutt. And Karen,

Stripes, and Poo-Poo all nodded in agreement.

"Yes, I know you did," said Stick Dog. "Tell me, what can each of you do that will distract the family while I take the hamburgers without them even noticing?"

"I can howl," said Mutt. "I am a world-class howler."

Then Stripes said, "I can jump really high. I can jump all over the place."

"I can chase my tail," said Karen. "Once, not very long ago, I actually caught it. It was so excellent."

"Great!" said Stick Dog. "All of those things are just great. And what about you, Poo-Poo? What kind of distraction can you provide?"

Poo-Poo thought about it long and hard. You could tell he wanted to come up with an

outstanding idea like the others. After pacing a few circles, Poo-Poo stopped. "I know," he said. "I can run face-first into a tree and only get hurt a little bit."

"Well," Stick Dog said, and stared at him for a moment. "That will certainly serve as a distraction, Poo-Poo. Great idea. Now, while all of you are distracting the family, I'll grab the hamburgers and take them back to my place for a fabulous feast."

All of the dogs nodded in agreement. Their mouths were starting to drool as they thought about those tasty hamburgers and how close—how very, very close—they were to getting them.

Chapter 9
SPIN, HOWL, BOUNCE, AND THUMP

They waited until the mom in the yellow apron took the hamburgers from the barbecue grill and set them on the picnic table. This was very important to Stick Dog. He did not want to snatch a bunch of hamburgers that were too hot to carry—or eat.

Do you know that feeling? It's a bad feeling. Like when you're really hungry and there's a nice slice of steaming hot cheese pizza right there in front of you—and you just can't wait. And then you take a bite and—ZAM!—you burn the roof of your mouth so badly that it makes a little flap of loose skin hang down, and you spend the rest of the day trying to tear that thing off with your tongue—only it takes forever, and it SLOWLY DRIVES YOU CRAZY until you'd do just about anything, INCLUDING STICKING A VACCUUM CLEANER'S SUCKING TUBE THINGY IN YOUR MOUTH, just to get it out!

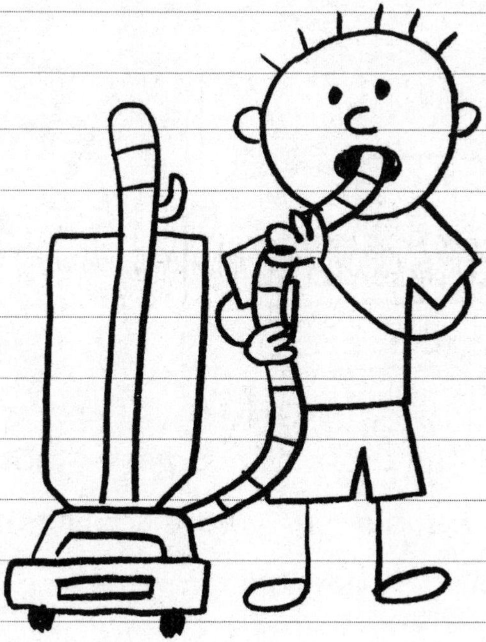

I really don't like it when that happens.

Anyway, all five dogs waited behind the honeysuckle bush until the hamburgers were off the grill and the mom and dad were finished setting the table. They called the boy and girl, who immediately picked up their soccer ball and came running to the gazebo. It appeared they were just as hungry as the dogs.

And those hamburgers—those delicious hamburgers—were cooling off to the perfect temperature. And the family—that no-good, selfish, rotten, stingy bunch of hamburger-munching humans—was just getting ready to eat.

It was then that the dogs put their plan into action. Just as the family was picking up their paper plates, from behind the honeysuckle bush ran five dogs they'd never seen before. When they heard barking, the family stopped putting food on their plates and turned to look.

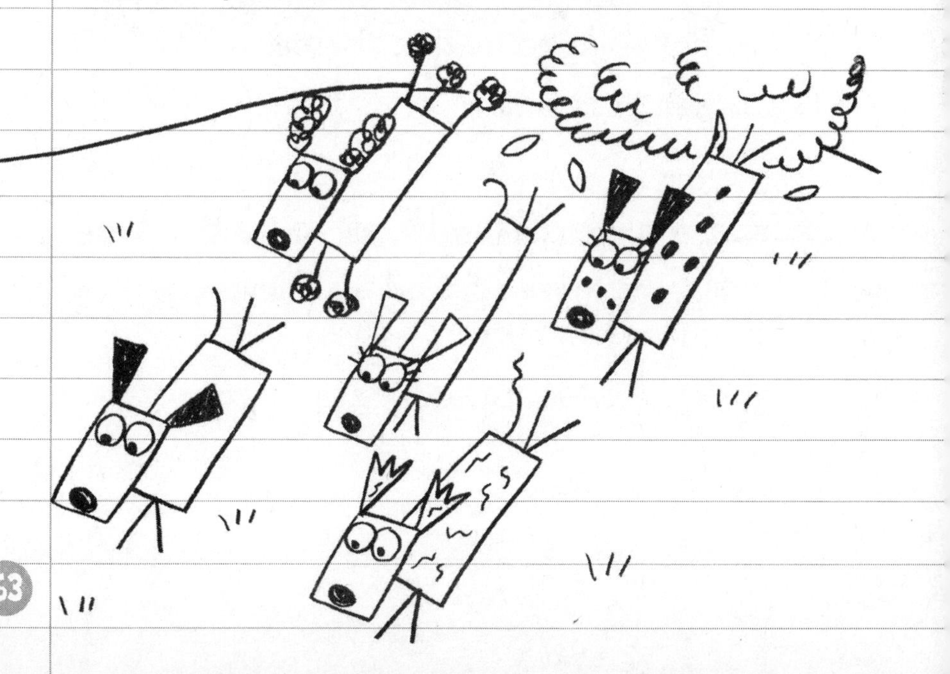

Now, they weren't quite alarmed or anything. It wasn't as if five rhinoceroses came charging out of the woods at them. Or five man-eating lions. Or five ooze-filled, orange aliens from the Planet DangerVille or something.

After all, these were just five dogs. And one of them was Karen, the dachshund. And, let's be honest, I don't care how ferocious a dachshund happens to be (and Karen isn't very ferocious at all), you're just not going to be that alarmed when you see one coming.

So it would probably be fair to say that the family was more startled than anything.

As the dogs got closer and closer, the

family stopped everything they were doing. The son stood as still as a statue, a square slice of cheddar cheese pinched between his pointer finger and thumb. The dad was frozen with his hand deep in a big bowl of crunchy potato chips. The daughter was holding a ketchup bottle—she just kept squeezing it and squeezing it. A bright red stream of ketchup was creating a great red mountain on the side of her paper plate, which was now getting lopsided and starting to tip over.

And the mom was staring with a dill pickle halfway in and halfway out of her mouth. In fact, it kind of looked like she was trying to take her temperature with the pickle. For a minute, you thought she was going to pull it out, look at it, and declare, "Yay! The pickle says my temperature is only ninety-eight point six degrees! Let's eat!"

When the dogs reached the gazebo, the family was still staring. The dogs were panting. The sun was shining. And the show—the, ahem, distractions—were all about to begin. And when they began, things happened very, very fast.

Karen was the first one to grab the family's attention. She started turning in a circle right next to the picnic table, chasing her tail with terrific determination and skill.

She started slowly at first and then built up greater and greater momentum.

It was only a matter of eight or nine seconds before she reached supreme tail-chasing velocity. The sound of her nails clattering against the concrete floor echoed inside the gazebo. Karen turned round and round and round until she was just this brown, spinning, blurry whirlwind.

You couldn't tell where her head was—or her body or her tail. They all blended together.

Just when they thought she couldn't go any faster, Karen doubled her speed. Each of the family members now felt a strong, whirling wind blow across their ankles. The dad's pants began to rustle and flap.

She was Karen, the Doggie Tornado.

And, boy, did the family look at her. Their eyes darted back and forth, trying to make heads or tails—quite literally—of what they were looking at. Their mouths hung open in wonder. In fact, a big chunk of the dill pickle that was halfway in and halfway out of the mom's mouth fell down to the ground during the commotion. The rest was still dangling from her lips. Stick Dog thought about running in and picking it up; but he knew his first priority was hamburgers, so he left it alone.

They all stared at Karen until a loud, roaring, piercing sound came from the other side of the picnic table.

It was Mutt. And, man, could he howl.

The family turned

from Karen, the Doggie Tornado, to stare at Mutt, the Canine Howling Machine. And as they snapped their heads around to see where the deafening roar was coming from, all four family members slapped their hands over their ears.

This was an instinctive response for any human to make to this mind-numbing sound. It was also an especially unfortunate response for the daughter. In the midst of all the chaos, you see, she had forgotten there was a ketchup bottle in her right hand. So she got a sharp jab to her face with the plastic bottle—and a great red ketchup splotch on her right cheek. Mutt's massive howl was so loud, though, that a ketchup splotch seemed a small price to pay for the ability to cover her ears.

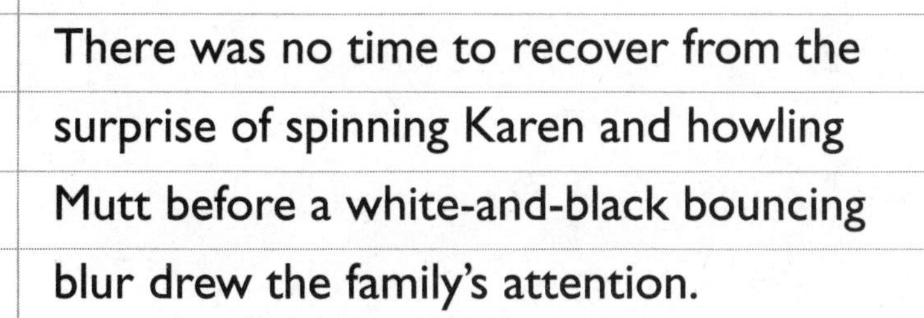

There was no time to recover from the surprise of spinning Karen and howling Mutt before a white-and-black bouncing blur drew the family's attention.

It was, as I'm sure you know, Stripes.

Imagine a white Super Ball—like the kind you buy for a quarter from a bubble gum–type machine at the grocery store or the Laundromat—with black spots. Then imagine firing that ball with all your might inside that gazebo.

Now you have an exact idea of what Stripes looked like.

She was jumping and bouncing everywhere. Off benches. Off tables. Off the other dogs. Off each human's shoes, ankles, and knees.

Stripes bounced one way, and her shoulder slammed into the picnic table. She bounced off the picnic table and banged into the gazebo wall. She bounced off the gazebo wall and smashed into the dad's knee.

When she smashed into his knee, the father's hip rammed into the table, and the potato chip bowl popped up and flipped in the air. A spray of salty chips came raining down inside the gazebo. Many of the chips landed on the dad's head.

Stick Dog considered making a dash into the gazebo to gather all the spilled chips, but he knew his job was to get the hamburgers.

The humans whipped their heads back and

forth, up and down, watching Stripes go crazy. For a moment, it looked as if their heads might pop right off their bodies.

And I think their heads really might have popped off if it hadn't been for what happened next.

Even with their hands covering their ears, the family could hear the loud padding of four paws getting faster and faster—and then a great *THUMP!*

I bet you know who it was.

It was Poo-Poo.

Do you remember when you were a one-year-old? Probably not. It's hard to remember back that far. Besides, who wants to anyway? Do you want to have memories of drooling all over the place and grown-ups talking to you like you're a one-year-old? Well, you *were* a one-year-old, of course, but that doesn't mean they have to talk to you like that. You know what I mean? Goo-goo. Ga-ga. Blah-blah-blah. GROW UP, PEOPLE!

Anyway, when you were a one-year-old and just learning to walk, you would stumble and trip all over the place. You would bang your head into walls and smash your face on the floor when you fell. Don't be ashamed; we all did it. And here's the thing: When you got up, you almost always smiled anyway, because you had just taken some steps. You were learning to be an amazing, incredible, WALKING HUMAN! Who cares if your face is all bashed up?! You are walking like nobody's business! You thought: I bet nobody has ever done this in the entire history of the world!

Except, of course, in the whole history of the world, just about all of us have done it. But what the heck. You didn't know that at the time. So you were just pleased as all get out. You were an awesome Walking Machine!

Well, when Poo-Poo raced across the field and ran face-first into the tree trunk, that's sort of what he looked like. His legs were a little wobbly, his head

was a little hurt, but he was proud—so proud—of causing such a great distraction.

The family had stopped watching anything else. They just stared at Poo-Poo running into that tree again and again.

And Stick Dog knew that it was his turn. He had to do his job. He had to grab those hamburgers.

Chapter 10
PRAISE AND ATTENTION

Stick Dog was proud of his friends. They had done exactly what they were supposed to do. And the result was exactly what he'd planned—the family was completely distracted from the hamburgers.

It was time to snatch them.

Only here's the thing: he didn't grab the hamburgers.

They were right there in front of him on the picnic table. Oooh, they smelled so delicious too. He could just reach out with his mouth, grip the rim of the serving dish that the hamburgers were sitting in, and take them all the way back to the big empty pipe beneath Highway 16.

The family was distracted. Mutt, Poo-Poo,

Stripes, and Karen had all done their jobs perfectly. But Stick Dog did not grab the hamburgers.

Here's why: he didn't have to.

That's because the family of humans finally started moving. The dad went to Stripes and began scratching her under the chin, calming her Super Ball bouncing. He fed her a few potato chips that he picked out of his hair.

The mom went to Karen, scratched her tummy, and gave her the last bite of dill pickle. Karen stopped spinning, although she still wobbled a bit as she ate it.

The boy did something quite unusual. He ran over to Mutt, lifted his own chin in the air, and started howling himself. And, between you and me, that boy was a pretty good howler. He wasn't as good a howler as Mutt, of course. I'm not sure anybody is. But this kid was pretty good.

Mutt was so surprised that he stopped howling and listened to the boy instead—

which, if you think about it, is kind of a funny role reversal. The boy shared his piece of cheddar cheese with Mutt and then they started howling together.

Meanwhile, the girl sprinted right over to Poo-Poo, who was sitting in a daze next to the big tree trunk he had just rammed his head into. The girl began stroking Poo-Poo's head, and he collapsed comfortably into her lap. She leaned down to rub his head, and Poo-Poo licked a bit of ketchup off her cheek.

Now, you might think that Stick Dog would be mad about all this. After all, the plan was to get the hamburgers and run away. And Mutt, Poo-Poo, Stripes, and Karen were definitely not running away.

But here's something you may not know: There are two things that dogs like even more than food.

Do you know what they are?

Praise and attention. And in this case, the family was giving the four dogs all the praise and attention they could handle.

Think about it. If you came home from school with a big A+ on an important quiz, what would you want your parents to say?

"Here, have an apple."

Or

"Great job. I know how hard you worked to earn this grade. I'm proud of you." And then they scratch your belly. Oh, okay, they don't really scratch your belly. You can scratch your own belly, after all. But you know what I mean, right?

Now, there's one more thing that you need to know before we get to the actual

hamburger part. And I bet you've been wondering about it, haven't you?

You've been wondering about Stick Dog himself, right? After all, he wasn't in on the distraction part of the plan.

Don't worry, he's fine.

Stick Dog is fine because he did what all good dogs do when there is praise and attention being dished out. He went around to each member of that family and got a little praise and attention for himself.

And do you know what happened next?

The mom and the dad went over to the serving dish full of hamburgers on the picnic table. They put five of those delicious hamburgers on paper plates and set them down on the ground.

So Poo-Poo, Mutt, Karen, Stripes, and Stick Dog all got a big hamburger each.

Between bites, Stick Dog said to his friends, "You know, these humans aren't so bad after all." He munched until the hamburger was all the way gone. He licked the plate clean.

Then the girl from the family did something truly spectacular.

She put another hamburger on his plate.

And patted his head.

The End

(until the next stomach grumbles).

Acknowledgments

I write with only Elizabeth and Jacob in mind. I can't believe they haven't gotten entirely sick of my jokes yet.

Special thanks to Margaret Anastas (my favorite advocate) and David Linker for finding me in Chicago—and for finding Stick Dog in his pipe below Highway 16. Additional thanks to Luana Horry for her good insights—and healthy breakfast choices. And thanks to Annie Stone and Nicole Hoff for answering my dumb questions.

Thanks to Doug Stewart for helping me navigate my way through the process—such a great help.

Thanks to Rob Brookman for being a great sounding board. Thanks to Diane Pletka for making so many things I've worked on look better. Thanks to Nikola Wilensky and Steve Spatz at BookBaby for early support.

Every student has a teacher who provided important guidance at an important time. Thanks to Mary Pierce Brosmer for being that teacher for me.

The following people have played a role in helping me along the way—and Stick Dog wouldn't have come to life without their help: Kate Cunningham, Burt Glass, Tom Schutte, Tom Bowman, Scott Nice, George Ventus, Wendy Pick, Scott Paschal, Lisa Schrag, the Ponce family, Beth Masterson, Myra Wagner, Jayne Krulewitch, Jane Lomar, Eric Mizuno, Becky Schifra, Peter Lechman, and Bob Listernick.

A quick message to Richard, Carol, Jim, Donna, Tom, Susie, Soo, Nancy, Rob, Bud, Liz, Sarah, Mo, Tom, Kate, Mike, and Misty: You may or may not think that the characters in this book are based on you. You may or may not be right. If you are right, I would like to make one thing perfectly clear: I'm Stick Dog.

Oh, I forgot. I want to say "Hi" to Stephanie Ponce.

Hi, Stephanie.